The Ninjabread Man

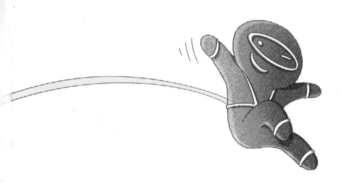

by Katrina Charman

and Fabiano Fiorin

W
FRANKLIN WATTS
LONDON•SYDNEY

This story is based on the traditional fairy tale,
The Gingerbread Man, but with a new twist.
You can read the original story in
Must Know Stories. Can you make
up your own twist for the story?

Franklin Watts
First published in great Britain in 2015 by The Watts Publishing Group

Text © Katrina Charman 2015
Illustrations © Fabiano Fiorin 2015

The rights of Katrina Charman to be identified as the author
and Fabiano Fiorin as the illustrator of this Work have been asserted
in accordance with the Copyright, Designs and Patents Act, 1988.

ISBN 978 1 4451 3841 1 (hbk)
ISBN 978 1 4451 3964 7 (pbk)
ISBN 978 1 4451 3966 1(library ebook)
ISBN 978 1 4451 3965 4 (ebook)

Series Editor: Melanie Palmer
Series Advisor: Catherine Glavina
Series Designer: Peter Scoulding
Cover Designer: Cathyrn Gilbert

Printed in China

Franklin Watts
An imprint of
Hachette Children's Group
Part of The Watts Publishing Group
Carmelite House
50 Victoria Embankment
London EC4Y 0DZ

An Hachette UK Company
www.hachette.co.uk

www.franklinwatts.co.uk

Once upon a time, in a small house in the forest, a lonely old man decided to make himself a friend. So he baked a gingerbread ninja: a Ninjabread man.

But when the Ninjabread man turned golden brown, he jumped up and ran out the door.

"Stop!" yelled the old man,
chasing after him.

But the Ninjabread man kept running, shouting: "Ka-Pow! Hi-Yah! And Shazam! You can't catch me, I'm the Ninjabread man."

Along the path, a hungry pig was sniffing for acorns beneath the mud. He saw the delicious Ninjabread man and shouted: "Stop, I want to eat you!"

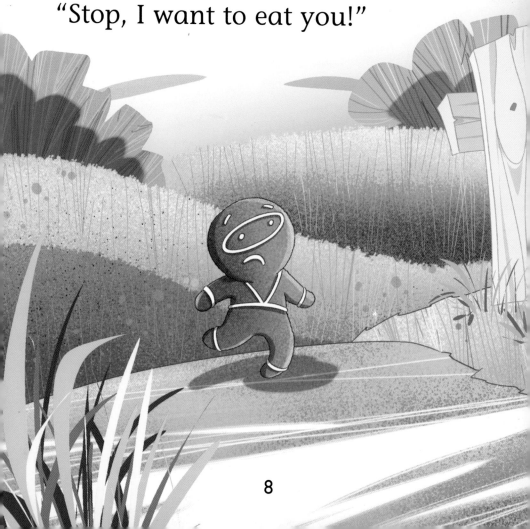

The Ninjabread man twisted out of the way, singing: "Ka-Pow! Hi-Yah! And Shazam! You can't catch me, I'm the Ninjabread man."

At the edge of the forest, a herd of cows grazed in a field.

One of them spotted the yummy Ninjabread man and squeezed through the fence.

"Stop! I want to eat you!" it cried.

14

The Ninjabread man rolled
right over the cow's back.
"Ka-Pow! Hi-Yah! And Shazam!
You can't catch me, I'm the
Ninjabread man."

Further down the hill, a flock of chicks pecked at the ground looking for grain. One by one, they smelled the Ninjabread man as he whirled and twirled towards them.

"Stop! We want to eat you!"
They rushed towards him with
their hungry beaks

But the Ninjabread man
backflipped over them.
"Ka-Pow! Hi-Yah! And Shazam!
You can't catch me, I'm the
Ninjabread man," he chuckled.

Then he reached a deep, wide river. He searched for a way across without getting soggy.

A crafty fox was watching.
"I'll help you cross the river," he
said. "Just climb onto my back."

"STOP!" yelled the old man who had finally caught up. "I can teach you to jump this river in one single bound."

The Ninjabread man laughed. "Ha, ha! I don't need help from anyone! I'm the Ninjabread man!"

He took a flying leap but missed the bank, landing on a drooping tree branch.

To his surprise, the old man leapt across the water, grabbing the Ninjabread man's arm and taking him safely to the other side.

"Wow!" gasped the Ninjabread man. "Can you teach me those moves?" The old man nodded.

Soon the Ninjabread man was
the star of Ninja school. He learnt
how to jump rivers ... and avoid
hungry foxes!

Puzzle 1

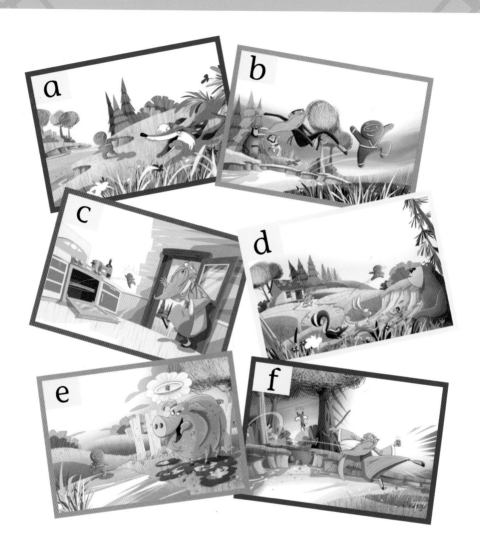

Put these pictures in the correct order.
Which event do you think is most important?
Now try writing the story in your own words!

Puzzle 2

1. I can flip and jump!

2. I love baking biscuits.

3. I have big jaws!

4. I don't always tell the truth.

5. I can teach Ninja!

6. I do not know how to swim!

Choose the correct speech bubbles for each character. Can you think of any others? Turn over to find the answers.

Answers

Puzzle 1

The correct order is: 1c, 2d, 3e, 4a, 5f, 6b

Puzzle 2

The old man: 2, 5

The Ninjabread man: 1, 6

The fox: 3, 4

Look out for more Hopscotch Twisty Tales

The Lovely Duckling
ISBN 978 1 4451 1633 4

Hansel and Gretel
and the Green Witch
ISBN 978 1 4451 1634 1

The Emperor's New Kit
ISBN 978 1 4451 1635 8

Rapunzel and the
Prince of Pop
ISBN 978 1 4451 1636 5

Dick Whittington
Gets on his Bike
ISBN 978 1 4451 1637 2

The Pied Piper and
the Wrong Song
ISBN 978 1 4451 1638 9

The Princess and the
Frozen Peas
ISBN 978 1 4451 0675 5

Snow White Sees the Light
ISBN 978 1 4451 0676 2

The Elves and the
Trendy Shoes
ISBN 978 1 4451 0678 6

The Three Frilly Goats Fluff
ISBN 978 1 4451 0677 9

Princess Frog
ISBN 978 1 4451 0679 3

Rumpled Stilton Skin
ISBN 978 1 4451 0680 9

Jack and the Bean Pie
ISBN 978 1 4451 0182 8

Brownilocks and the Three
Bowls of Cornflakes
ISBN 978 1 4451 0183 5

Cinderella's Big Foot
ISBN 978 1 4451 0184 2

Little Bad Riding Hood
ISBN 978 1 4451 0185 9

Sleeping Beauty –
100 Years Later
ISBN 978 1 4451 0186 6

The Three Little Pigs &
the New Neighbour
ISBN 978 1 4451 0181 1